World's Most Terrifying "True" Ghost Stories

Arthur Myers

Illustrated by Jim Sharpe

Sterling Publishing Co., Inc. New York

To Virginia Ritchie Cutler

Library of Congress Cataloging-in-Publication Data

Myers, Arthur.
World's most terrifying "true" ghost stories / Arthur Myers ; illustrated by Jim Sharpe.
p. cm.
Includes index.
Summary: Presents thirty-three brief, purportedly true stories featuring ghosts and other supernatural phenomena.
ISBN 0-8069-1350-9
1. Ghosts—juvenile literature. [1. Ghosts. 2. Supernatural.] I. Sharpe, Jim, ill. II. Title.
BF1461.M935 1995
133.1—dc20
95-12612
CIP
AC

10 9 8 7 6 5 4 3 2 1

Published by Sterling Publishing Company, Inc.
387 Park Avenue South, New York, N.Y. 10016

Distributed in Canada by Sterling Publishing
℅ Canadian Manda Group, One Atlantic Avenue, Suite 105
Toronto, Ontario, Canada M6K 3E7
Distributed in Great Britain and Europe by Cassell PLC
Wellington House, 125 Strand, London WC2R 0BB, England
Distributed in Australia by Capricorn Link (Australia) Pty Ltd.
P.O. Box 6651, Baulkham Hills, Business Centre, NSW 2153, Australia
Manufactured in the United States of America

Sterling ISBN 0-8069-1350-9

CONTENTS

1. **Ghost Around the House** 5
The Haunted Cleaning Lady
A Very Bothersome Ghost
A Wild and Crazy Lady Ghost
Something Black and Cold

2. **Haunted Places** 19
The Haunted Museum
A Very Firm Disbeliever
The Tale of a Thief
A Very Strange Telephone Call

3. **Strange!** 31
The Dog Who Was Scared to Death by a Ghost
The Disembodied Arm
The Pilot Who Saw a Dread Future
The Man Who Wasn't There

4. **Messages from Ghosts** 41
A Call from Uncle Andy
Help from a Ghost
The Ghost of a Deformed Monk
A Terrifying Visitor
Monkeys in the Closet

5. Poltergeists? Or Something Else? 53
When Is a Ghost Not a Ghost?
A Fatal Apparition
Pebbles from Heaven

6. Malicious Ghosts 61
A Dangerous Spirit
A Very Scary Doll
The Demonic Hairdresser
The Ghost Who Hated Women

7. Ghosts Who Stay Behind 71
The Lady and the Time Warp
When Battles Replay Themselves
A Hitchhiking Ghost
The Hotel Clerk Who Won't Quit
A Sight Not on the Program

8. Betrayal and Murder 83
The Ghost Who Came Back for Justice
The Silent Witness
The Party Stopper
The Waltz of Death

Index 95

1. GHOST AROUND THE HOUSE

* She tried to clean the house—but the ghosts kept messing it up . . .

* A ghost steals clothes and food . . .

* A wild woman ghost takes possession of a young actress . . .

* A cold, billowy, black shape tries to wrap a woman in its arms . . .

The Haunted Cleaning Lady

Ghosts abound on Nantucket Island, off the coast of Massachusetts, as they do on many places near the water. One theory is that the damp atmosphere makes it easier for spirits to transfer their energy to us living people. "Your mind is electrical," is the way one psychic puts it, "and what is the best conductor of electricity? Water."

But although Margo Smith, as a native of Nantucket, was no stranger to ghosts and stories of ghosts, when she took the job of cleaning Mrs. Deauville's house, it got to be just too much, although she stuck it out for quite a while. Her employer was away a lot, so during Margo's weekly cleaning chores she usually was alone in the house.

"On my first day at work," Margo recalls, "I brought my dog with me. He hopped out of the truck, ran up to the front door, and then wouldn't set foot inside."

He wouldn't go in the front door; he wouldn't go in the back door. She couldn't pull, push or carry him in. He had never done that at any other house. Margo thought to herself, "Oh no, here we go. There's something here."

The spirits—there seemed to be several—started playing with the phone. The first day, Margo was vacuuming when she heard the phone beeping as though someone had just taken it off the hook. She looked, and sure enough, the phone was off the hook.

Okay, she said to herself, I can deal with it. Then, as she was vacuuming, she heard the sound of a group of people, talking and laughing. She turned the vacuum off, and the house was dead silent. She turned the vacuum back on, and the party sounds started again, the high and low voices of women and men talking.

They were just warming up.

After a few weeks, the furniture began to move around. If Margo was upstairs, she'd hear furniture dragged around downstairs. She'd gallop down the stairs and find that chairs and tables *had* been moved around.

These things happened only when she was alone in the house, when Mrs. Deauville and her family and guests were somewhere else. Perhaps Margo was a particularly psychic person, with whom the spirits knew they could communicate—and tease.

She never actually saw things being moved—only the results. "I was trying to straighten up and clean," she says, "and they were messing things up as fast as I could put them in order."

Margo never mentioned these happenings to Mrs. Deauville. She left it to her employer to bring up, if she wanted to, and she never did.

The spirits began to step up the pace. One day Margo was vacuuming under a bed, and something grabbed the front of the vacuum. It gave a little, as though something were holding on to it. When Margo pulled hard, the vacuum came loose from the hose and remained under the bed. After a considerable period of debate with herself, Margo worked up the courage to look under the bed. There was nothing there but the vacuum attachment. After another period of convincing herself there was nothing to be afraid of—hah!—Margo forced herself to reach under the bed and grab it.

Margo tried to reason with the ghosts. She'd open the front door and call, "Hello, I'm here. I'll be as quick as I can."

She didn't have much success. Furniture kept moving. Once, after a particularly long period of rumbling, she ran downstairs, to find all the living room chairs arranged in a circle.

Finally it got to be too much, even for Margo, the native Nantuckian. Pictures started coming down off the walls. Dishes clattered in the kitchen. A rug flew through the air and struck Margo in the back.

"I also got whacked," says Margo, "by some sofa pillows that zipped across the room on their own. Finally, a chair was thrown at me. It missed me, but that did it!"

Margo resigned.

A Very Bothersome Ghost

Some ghosts are rather intriguing to have around the house. They water the flowers, or bring in pleasant fragrances such as chocolate or baking bread, or something else they were associated with during life. Other ghosts, however, can be absolutely pesky—nobody you would want around, alive or dead.

An example of the pesky kind comes from Nollamara, a town in Western Australia.

Around 1970, Lee and Pat Decker and their baby son moved into one of the oldest houses in town. Lee had gone into business for himself and had bought expensive equipment for his new factory.

The day after they moved in, they found a plain, sealed envelope in their letter box, containing ten dollars.

A few days later, Pat was dusting a window frame and

a twenty-dollar bill fluttered down from the curtains. She spent the money.

When the couple went to bed one night, they found five ten-dollar bills strewn across the bed.

Lee refused to use this mysterious money. He said that, when he lived in Indonesia, he had heard of evil spirits who would leave money around to tempt people. The Deckers put the money in a cupboard. When they left the house for a while, they came back to find that the money had disappeared.

The ghost had some definitely annoying habits, however. One time all of Pat's clothes were removed from a closet and scattered across the floor of the bedroom. Sometimes articles of clothing disappeared. Sometimes they reappeared; some were gone for good.

The ghost would often take Lee's cigarettes, and sometimes pepper him with paper pellets while he was reading his newspaper. Once, though, when Lee complained, a new pack of cigarettes appeared on the kitchen table.

The ghost often stole food. Apples, pears, and cooked legs of chicken vanished. On the plus side, the ghost would occasionally wash dishes—although it rarely got them back on the right shelves.

One time the ghost stole a steak that Pat was preparing for Lee's lunch. She was so angry that she shouted at the ghost, and a few minutes later the steak reappeared on the plate.

The Deckers brought in clergymen to try to rid the place of the ghost, but they had little success.

The ghost's identity was not considered too much of a mystery in Nollamara. A man named Tom had formerly lived in the house, and had become very dejected after the death of his wife. He had committed suicide by hanging himself at the rear of the building.

The Deckers held a séance, and contacted a woman named Jean who had died in the house, presumably Tom's wife. But it didn't help. Soon after this, the Deckers moved out.

The house was demolished, leaving the newspapers in the area deprived of a subject that had fascinated their readers for many months.

A Wild and Crazy Lady Ghost

When Susan Strasberg, a well-known young actress, bought a house in Beverly Hills, California, she became a bit troubled. Her husband kept seeing a lady ghost around the house.

"Christopher was an actor and a bit eccentric," she would say jokingly. "But when he would talk to this lady and invite her to dance with him, it would give me the chills."

Susan became even more nervous when a physician friend, a quite level-headed young woman, visited her. After her first night, the friend related at breakfast that something had held her down in bed for a few minutes. She had the impression it was a woman.

Then Susan got a call from a friend who said he was

sitting with a man who used to live in the house. The man wanted to know how was the lady.

"What lady?" asked Susan.

"The lady who haunts the house," her friend replied.

"I wish you hadn't told me this," Susan said.

She began to get really scared. "I had candles burning, and Bibles, and Jewish stars, and Buddhas," she says. "I wasn't taking any chances."

Susan had recently been in a film in Italy, where her stand-in had been a tiny young woman named Marina DeYorzo. They had become close friends.

"When this little girl and I walked down the street," Susan says, "the people thought she was a witch. They'd make a protective sign. They're very superstitious in Bari, the southern tip of Italy. Marina was almost an albino, and that made them think she was psychic, which to them would be a witch. She *was* very psychic, very open to other realities."

Soon after, Marina came to visit Susan in Beverly Hills. One day the two of them were doing yoga breathing, which can alter consciousness. Two male friends of Susan's husband were also in the room.

Suddenly, Susan relates, "Marina started to say in that strange accent—like Marlene Dietrich—'Wiolet, I see wiolet. How beautiful!' Then her tone changed to terror, and she cried, 'Oh, there's a woman! She's coming towards me! She's trying to possess me, she's trying to take over my body . . . ' "

The men felt they had to get Marina out of the house, but she had a sudden ferocious strength. They could not hold her. She struck them over and over, bruising and scratching them.

Susan desperately phoned people for advice. She was

sprinkling salt, saying the Lord's prayer, doing everything she had ever read or heard of.

"Marina had the strength of ten men," Susan says. "She was moaning and going through convulsions."

They finally managed to drag her out the front door. The instant she crossed the threshold, she stopped struggling and said, "What are you holding me for? Put me down!"

When they told her what had happened, she wanted to go back into the house. She wasn't going to let the ghost intimidate her.

Susan vetoed that idea. She packed suitcases and they moved to a hotel until Marina left.

Susan brought in psychics, priests, Indian mystics to try to clear the house, but she doesn't believe they were successful.

Her husband would catch glimpses of the ghost, and a guest reported one morning that something had held her down in bed momentarily.

"I never found out who the ghost was," Susan says.

Something Black and Cold

It started with little things, strange incidents that were sometimes inconvenient, sometimes almost amusing. But then the heavy trouble began, and the terror.

In the early 1970s, two sisters, Lois Dean and Diantha Summer, moved their families into two old houses in the middle of Rawlins, Wyoming, a small city in the Rocky Mountains. Lois and her husband and their six children moved into the big house. Diantha and her two sons took the carriage house right behind.

Very soon, strange things started happening in the big house.

* Lights kept turning on and off. At first, the adults thought it was just the kids playing around. But they soon found that lights seemed to be going on or off by themselves, when no one was around. Lois and her husband had the big house rewired, but it kept happening.

* When the children were playing games, they would leave the room for a moment and come back to find pieces missing.

* An older daughter found the colors of her makeup often ran together. At first, she thought the younger children were doing it, but she padlocked her bedroom and it kept happening.

* The family dog wagged his tail as though at an invisible guest, and his eyes followed something across the room.

* Sometimes in the big house the bathroom cabinet would be found completely empty. Toothbrushes, combs and medicines would be gone, to be found later in odd places. Again, Lois thought it was the children, but it happened when they were at school and she was alone in the house.

Then things began to get rough.

A boyfriend of one of the girls was playfully climbing through a window. Something unseen picked him up and threw him inside, up against the wall. That was the end of that boyfriend. He never came back for another visit.

Not long afterward, one of the younger boys said he thought he had seen something in the garage. Mike, Diantha's 14-year-old son, decided to take a look. He started out the back door of the big house and suddenly felt two hands grab him and throw him through the air, back into the kitchen against the refrigerator. He had red marks on his chest as though something had scratched him.

Lois was infuriated. She began yelling, "I don't care who you are, I'm not putting up with you coming into my house and hurting kids!"

So angry that she was momentarily unafraid, she dashed out into the garage. There she saw a black shape.

"It was big and billowy," she says, "and it was dressed like a woman in something black and long."

It came toward her smoothly, as though it were on wheels.

"Something black and cold started coming out of it, like ribbons," she recalls. "It started wrapping me in those strands. I could feel their coldness. I could not move."

Then she felt her sister, who saw the shape too, grab her from behind and jerk her away from the thing and back to the big house.

The sisters sat up all night, praying as hard as they could. The prayers may have had a good effect, for they never saw the thing again.

They took to calling that incident "the main event." Afterward, they felt the atmosphere to be a little less oppressive. However, everyone had a sense that the place was still not quite right, and before long both families moved out.

What on earth was happening there? Lois feels she got a strong clue when she talked with an aged aunt who had lived in the neighborhood in the early 1900s.

"She told me," Lois says, "that there had been a graveyard on that property, and the bodies were dug up and moved to a larger cemetery somewhere else in town. But there was talk that two bodies had been left behind."

Was that the answer? Throughout the world there have been many, many reports of cemeteries dug up and moved. And if there are bodies left behind, the spirits who once resided in them are thought to become restless and make their presence known to those of us who are still alive.

2. HAUNTED PLACES

* A museum houses some very active spirits . . .

* A Mississippi mansion is host to a phantom who plays Chopin on a very real piano . . .

* A grave should never be disturbed, as one young man learns—to his horror . . .

* A phone call from another world?

The Haunted Museum

One of the favorite public haunted places in Toronto, Canada, is a museum called the Mackenzie House, but the people who work there don't seem to enjoy it as much as casual visitors. In fact, the people who take care of the place often find it pretty scary.

The house was once the home of William Mackenzie, who was at one time the mayor of Toronto, but he made so many enemies that for a time he had to flee Canada and take refuge in the United States.

Now that he is safely dead, he seems to have returned to his Toronto home. Some caretakers have seen him.

One, a Mrs. Edmunds, tells of seeing the apparition of a small, bald man in an old-fashioned frock coat. This certainly sounds like Mackenzie, although in life he usually wore a red wig. Perhaps he has mislaid it in the next world. Or maybe he has become less vain about his appearance.

Mackenzie published a small newspaper, and the press on which he printed it is still in the cellar. It is kept locked, but many staff members swear they have heard rumbling below that sounds suspiciously like an old-time printing press going full tilt.

Another ghost, more belligerent toward the living than Mackenzie, is that of a woman. Mrs. Edmunds has had her problems with this one. She tells of awakening at night to see a woman with dark brown hair and a narrow face, leaning over and staring at her intently. A few months later, Mrs. Edmunds awoke again to see the ghostly woman. This time the ghost struck her in the face, giving her a black eye.

The Edmunds children keep seeing the ghost of a woman in the bathroom, a ghost that disappears on being sighted. Plants in the house are often watered mysteriously—and sometimes carelessly, for the curtains are splashed with mud.

It's not on record exactly how long the Edmunds put up with these shenanigans before moving out. However, it *is* on record that other caretakers have also had their troubles. Many have reported that the toilets flushed by themselves, and that water taps turned on when there was no one—alive—around to do this.

A caretaker named Mrs. McCleary says she often feels as though a ghost is putting its arms around her. However, since the spirit remains invisible, it's anyone's guess whether it is Mackenzie or the lady ghost.

Whenever renovation work is done at the house, workmen come up with a whole new batch of anecdotes about the place. Often objects such as sawhorses, ropes and drop sheets are found in the morning to have been moved around, even though the building had been locked all night. And one workman, Murdo MacDonald, gained fame when he was first into the house one morning and found a hangman's noose over a stairway.

It's no wonder that the Mackenzie House is one of the favorite stops on Halloween ghost tours in Toronto.

A Very Firm Disbeliever

A wealthy young couple had built a large, elaborate house near Gulfport in Mississippi. Their teenage daughter committed suicide there. The parents were, of course, extremely sorrowful. But only a few days later, they fled the house taking a minimum of clothing, never to return.

Their hasty departure did not suggest sorrow as much as it did extreme fear. Rumors quickly spread that the house was now haunted.

Fran Franklin, now a professor of journalism at the University of Arkansas, was nine years old at the time. She had a favorite aunt, Harriet Gibbons, who was an unusual person. Tiny—only four feet tall—she was the editor of a daily newspaper in Mississippi, and she had very definite opinions. She knew the young couple, and ridiculed their flight as pure superstition.

"There is no such thing as a ghost," Harriet often said.

She said she planned to stay in the house overnight to prove there was nothing to be frightened of. Fran asked if she could go along, and her aunt agreed.

So one night, the two let themselves into the house with a key that Harriet had gotten from friends. They set two chairs in the front hallway and sat down to wait for something to happen. Around midnight, something happened.

Upstairs, they heard a door close. Then they heard what sounded like footsteps coming down the hall. Fran looked at the top of the wide staircase, expecting to see a ghostly figure, but she saw nothing. However, she could *hear* the footsteps coming down the stairs! As they reached the bottom of the stairs, Fran could see a depression in the carpet. When the footsteps reached the marble floor, they clicked across the foyer. They clicked down the hall to a set of double doors that opened into a music room. The doors opened.

Fran was terrified. She looked at her little aunt for a cue. Harriet sat unmoving, her face expressionless.

The footsteps continued across the floor of the music room, stopping at a piano that was visible from the foyer. As Fran and Harriet watched, the piano stool came back. The top covering the piano keys was raised, revealing the keyboard. A short concert of three pieces by Chopin came from the piano.

Then the music stopped. The cover of the keyboard came back down. The piano stool moved back to its original position.

The sound of steps came out of the room. The double doors closed. The steps tapped back across the marble foyer to the foot of the stairs. There they hesitated, as though the unseen performer was momentarily observing her audience of two. Then the footsteps went back up the stairs, and back down the upstairs hall. Fran and her aunt heard a door upstairs close.

Aunt Harriet turned to Fran. "It's time to go now," she said.

As they were driving back to their motel, Fran got up the courage to ask Aunt Harriet what she thought of all this.

"There is no such thing as a ghost," Aunt Harriet replied.

The Tale of a Thief

Charlie Sennett was an easygoing cowpoke, a good man to have along on a roundup or back in the bunkhouse. For he was an amusing fellow, always good for a story or a comradely laugh. He told most of his tales with a chuckle and a wink.

But there was one story he rarely told. And when he did tell it, he never laughed or winked. He stared intently into the fire as though he saw his fate there, and didn't like it one bit. People wondered why Charlie told the story at all. Some said he did it to humble himself, to make amends for something of which he was very much ashamed.

Charlie was born in Wyoming and lived and punched cattle there all his life. He had this experience, the most frightening of his life, when he was a young man of 19, in the year 1950.

The story involved a sacred Native American tradition. Charlie was well aware of what he was doing, for he was part Native American himself. And he couldn't excuse himself because he was young at the time. Native American children learn this custom very early in life.

The tradition is that a grave should never, never be disturbed.

Charlie knew of a kinsman who had been buried in a cave in an out-of-the-way canyon in a desolate area called Dinwoodie. The man, whose Native American name was Low Thunder, had been wealthy. He had owned much land and many cattle. Around his grave had been reverently placed his most prized possessions, for many Native Americans believed that a person's spirit could use these things in the next life. Charlie especially admired a splendid saddle that had been left beside the grave, so that Low Thunder could ride it in the Happy Hunting Grounds.

Charlie, a poor young man, had an old saddle so worn it was coming apart. He had just taken a new job at a ranch, and he hated to show up with this shabby saddle. He could not get his mind off the magnificent saddle at the grave of Low Thunder. After all, Charlie told himself, he had as much white blood as Native American. Why should he let himself be bound by superstition?

One day, when he found himself in the vicinity of the canyon, he made up his mind. He reined his horse into the canyon and climbed to the cave. He hesitated as he reached its mouth, telling himself it was not Low Thunder he was afraid of, but the rattlesnakes that swarmed in such caves. These live creatures, poisonous though they were, seemed less fearsome to him than an angry spirit. Encouraged, he plunged into the cave and quickly found the grave. There was the saddle, as beautiful as it had been when first placed there. He scooped it into his arms and ran. He pulled his old saddle off his horse, threw it over a cliff, put the saddle of Low Thunder on the horse and galloped away.

Far from the canyon, Charlie slowed his horse to a trot. Joy surged through him. No need to feel guilty, he told himself. How can you steal from the dead?

Suddenly he felt a thud behind him, as though someone had landed in the saddle! He heard a ghastly whisper in his ear. "Take back that saddle!" it hissed.

Charlie broke out in a cold sweat. He whipped his horse into a gallop, as though he could outrun whatever was clinging to him—as though he could leave that whisper behind.

But now the voice did not whisper. It roared, "Take back that saddle!" It bellowed, "Take back that saddle!"

His horse stumbled. It veered as though trying to turn. It twisted its head, eyes wide and huge. It was terrified. For animals are even more aware of spirits than humans are.

Charlie gave up. He whirled the horse around and sped back to the canyon. Uncinching the saddle, he raced into the cave and dropped it beside the grave. Then he leaped onto his frightened horse and rode off as though his life depended on it.

Miles away, he came to the lonely ranch of a friend. The man's wife is still alive, and she tells of Charlie's arrival that day. "He was riding bareback," she relates, "and he asked if he could borrow a saddle. I tried to give him dinner, but he broke down. He couldn't stop crying. He said he had stolen a saddle from a kinsman's grave. 'But I took it back,' he sobbed over and over, 'I took it back, I took it back . . . ' "

A Very Strange Telephone Call

Mammoth Cave National Park, in Kentucky, contains perhaps the most famous collection of caves in the world. According to many people who work there as guides, or who are among the 2,000,000 tourists who visit the caves each year, there are ghosts in those caverns.

The most convincing witnesses might well be members of the Cave Research Foundation, which numbers some 650 scientists who investigate caves all over the United States. Their headquarters are at Mammoth Park. Most CRF members are professors at universities, not the sort of people who would make up stories about ghostly experiences. But things happen. As one CRF member put it:

"We're a bunch of hard-nosed people. Most of us who have had these experiences are not believers in ghosts, ordinarily. We just describe the facts and let others decide."

Two CRF members who had a chilling experience are Dr. Will White, a professor of geochemistry at Pennsylvania State University, and Dr. George Deike, a government scientist. They were investigating Crystal Cave, which is no longer open to the public. However, it had once been open to tourists, and there was an old army field telephone down in the cave.

"I guess they used it," White says, "to let the guides know some people were coming, tell them to wake up."

On this day, White and Deike, on their way through the cave to do some geological exploration, were walking by this ancient, broken-down phone—when suddenly, it rang!

The two scientists were too startled, perhaps too fearful, to stop. They kept walking down the passageway.

White says, "When we got about 200 feet farther on, the phone rang again! We looked at each other for a moment, then we ran back. I picked up the old phone and answered. It was one of those old-fashioned army phones with a sort of butterfly switch on it.

"What I heard sounded like a phone sounds when it's off the hook and there are people in the room. You hear the sounds of voices, but you can't tell what they are saying. I said hello, or something like that. And on the other end there's a startled gasp. And that was all. No one responded. The line was now dead."

Astonished, the two scientists noticed that the phone was attached to a rusty, twisted phone line. They traced it back to the mouth of the cave, and out to a weathered shack that had once been a ticket office. But the phone line ended there. It was attached to nothing!

Had Dr. White heard the sounds of another world?

3. STRANGE!

* He was a trained attack dog—but he was frightened—to death!

* Grasped by a human hand—that stops at the elbow!

* It happened during World War II—a horrible vision of the future that came true . . .

* The man never left his sick bed, so what was it that got photographed in his place?

The Dog Who Was Scared to Death by a Ghost

They called him Chief, because he had once been owned by the police.

He belonged to the Iannucci family, who owned a restaurant in Glen Mills, Pennsylvania. The building had been an old farmhouse, built 250 years before, and they were rebuilding the old place.

As often happens when buildings are changed, it stirs up ghosts. They don't like changes. There was one especially frightening spirit. It threw vases and flashed lights off and on. Sometimes it appeared as a greyish form hovering over people in bed. But the living being that was most frightened by this ghost was Chief.

Jerry Iannucci had bought the dog from the police department in nearby Upper Darby. Chief's days were numbered, Jerry had heard, because Chief was so vicious and aggressive that he could not be controlled. The police were going to have to, as they put it, "terminate" him. Jerry figured that Chief would be perfect to have around the house to guard it while it was being renovated.

However, Jerry says, "The dog turned into a wimp as soon as he got here. There was something here that would cause him to creep around and cower in the corners."

One of the Iannucci sons, Rick, was living in the building, and Chief would constantly stay close by him. One night, however, Rick was away and the dog had to stay in the building by himself. Another son, Rob, arrived in the morning to do some work and found Chief obviously terrified.

"That dog was always freaked out here, from the moment we got him," Rob says. "He would completely shy away from certain areas of the building, and he especially stayed away from the third floor."

The third floor, called the "loft," was being restored as living quarters for some of the family.

When Rob arrived that morning, the dog followed him around, staying as close as possible. "He was really palling around with me," Rob says. "After a while I had to go up to the loft. I could see he didn't want to go up there, but he didn't want to be alone, so he finally followed me up the stairs. When we got up there, I started working on a bookcase at one end of a long room.

"The dog was acting very strange. He would freeze,

just stand stiffly and stare. You would think that somebody else was in the room. Then the dog started flinching. It was as though somebody was doing something to him. It was like something was standing next to him and threatening to hit him with a stick, or poking him. The dog started howling, and looking around wildly. He saw an open window and just dove through it, three stories above the ground. He was killed, of course."

"And," says Jerry Iannucci, "this was a dog who was so fierce that the police were going to shoot it."

The Disembodied Arm

Major MacGregor was a brave man. He had faced shot and shell and enemy soldiers in battle. But now he was terrified. This was something very different!

It was a night in 1871, and he was lying in bed in the elegant house of a cousin in Dublin, Ireland. He had been visiting his cousin when her husband became ill, and MacGregor had sat up with him several nights. But now the man seemed better, and MacGregor went to bed, asking a servant to call him if his host took a turn for the worse.

MacGregor, exhausted, fell asleep immediately. An hour later, he felt a push on his shoulder. He started up, thinking it was the servant.

"Is anything wrong?" he asked in the darkened room.

He got no answer, only another push.

The major got exceedingly annoyed. "Speak, man," he bellowed, "and tell me if anything is wrong!"

He still got no reply, but he had a feeling he was going to get another push. He twisted around in bed, reached out and grasped what seemed to be a human hand. It was warm and soft, a woman's hand.

"Who are you?" he demanded, but got no answer.

He tried to pull the hand towards him, but the owner of the hand seemed quite strong, and he was unable to.

Thoroughly irritated, MacGregor exclaimed, "I am determined to find out who you are!"

He held the hand tightly in his right hand, and with his left began to feel the wrist and arm. They seemed to be clothed in a tight-fitting sleeve, with a linen cuff.

When he got to the elbow, there was nothing more! All trace of the rest of the arm had disappeared! MacGregor was so astonished that he let go of the hand.

The next morning, he told of his strange experience. His hostess took his tale calmly.

His cousin said, "Oh, that was old Aunt Betty. She lived in the upper part of the house and died many years ago."

Aunt Betty had been a very nice person, she assured him, so there was nothing to worry about.

But when MacGregor talked with the servants, they were not so encouraging. Sometimes, they said, Aunt Betty's arm pulled the bedclothes off. One lady had received a slap in the face from an invisible hand.

MacGregor's cousin insisted that Aunt Betty would never think of hurting anyone. Maybe so, MacGregor reflected silently, but she just might scare you to death.

The Pilot Who Saw a Dread Future

Throughout history there has been evidence that at times some people have caught glimpses of the future. Often these pictures of approaching events come in dreams. But they are also seen by people who are fully awake. Take the experience of George Potter, a Royal Air Force pilot during World War II.

Wing Commander Potter was stationed at a base called RAF Shallufa in Egypt. From this base, bombing planes flew out over the Mediterranean Sea to plant torpedoes and mines in the paths of ships carrying supplies to the North African desert forces of the German General Erwin Rommel. This was a crucial period of the war, the first time the Allied armies were winning. They were pushing back the forces of the Germans' most successful general, known as the Desert Fox.

The airmen's missions were extremely dangerous. Between bombing runs there was much nervous gaiety as they tried to forget the peril of their lives. They ate, drank, sang and laughed as though they were schoolboys, which they had been not long before.

One evening, Commander Potter entered the Officers' Mess with a friend, Flying Officer Reg Lamb. At a nearby table, a group of flyers were celebrating something—perhaps that they were still alive. One of them was a wing commander whom Potter refers to as Roy.

After a few moments, Potter heard a loud burst of laughter from the table, and glanced over that way. As he has described it:

"I turned and saw the head and shoulders of Roy moving ever so slowly in a background of blue-blackness. His lips were drawn back from his teeth in a dreadful grin. He had no eyes in his eye sockets. The flesh of his face was blotched in greenish, purplish shadows."

A few seconds later, Potter felt Reg Lamb tugging at his sleeve. "What's the matter?" Lamb asked. "You've gone white as a sheet. You look as if you've seen a ghost!"

"I *have* seen a ghost," Potter replied. "Roy over there has the mark of death on him."

Lamb looked over at the table of joking officers, but could see nothing unusual.

That night Roy was shot down. He and his crew were

seen clambering into a life raft, but the air-sea rescue planes were unable to find them. The flyers were never heard from again.

"I then knew what I had seen," Potter relates. "The blue-black background was the sea at night, and Roy was floating in it, dead, with his head and shoulders held up by his life jacket."

The Man Who Wasn't There

Ghosts on photographs, although not an everyday occurrence, have been reported since the 1800s. But for a live person to appear on film when he or she was somewhere else when the photo was taken is even more unusual. The latter event has become something of a tourist attraction at the parliament headquarters in Victoria, Canada.

On January 13, 1865, the first legislative council of British Columbia was having its official picture taken. One member of the council, Charles Good, was seriously ill and confined to his bed at home. It must have been unbearably disappointing to Good to miss this historic occasion. However, he is in the picture! Everyone, including Good himself, was astonished when the photo was printed and Good's face appeared in the place he would have occupied had he been there. He looks a bit transparent, but he is there. This extraordinary picture still hangs in the halls of the British Columbian parliament.

It is known that people's astral bodies can travel with or without the person's being aware of it. Charles Good insisted that he was completely unaware of leaving his sickbed, but apparently part of him did—and had its picture taken!

4. MESSAGES FROM GHOSTS

* They both spoke to Uncle Andy on the phone, but Uncle Andy was dead . . .

* The race car driver knew he was facing imminent death, till he heard from his dad . . .

* A deformed monk reveals his murder . . .

* A soldier receives a frightening visit from his brother . . .

* Table tipping yields a very odd message!

A Call from Uncle Andy

The idea of phone calls from the dead may seem outlandish, but while they don't exactly clutter up the phone lines, they are not as uncommon as one might think. Many people have received calls that seem to come from another world.

Once such phone call was experienced by Ida Lupino, who was a movie star during the middle of the 20th century. Although Ida became famous in Hollywood, she had been born and brought up in England, a member of a theatrical family that went back for generations. Her father and mother, Stanley and Connie Lupino, were well-known performers in the English variety theater. When Ida was nine, they were living in London at her grandmother's house.

One night, Ida had a disturbing dream about a man

she called Uncle Andy, a friend of her parents. She woke up, and went downstairs to tell her grandmother, who was preparing a late supper for Stanley and Connie. While Ida was telling her grandmother about her dream, the phone rang. Her grandmother asked Ida to answer it.

"I went to the phone," Ida relates, "took it off the hook and heard a voice on the line. But it was so faint I could scarcely understand the words. Finally, the voice became stronger and I could understand the message, repeated monotonously several times: 'I must talk to Stanley. It is terribly important.' "

The little girl recognized the voice as that of Uncle Andy. She said her father wasn't home yet. But the voice kept saying the same thing over and over. Ida called her grandmother to the phone. She heard her grandmother say, "Andy, are you *ill*? I'll ask Stanley to call you the moment he comes in."

Then the call was cut off. Ida's grandmother protested angrily to the operator, who insisted there had not been a call on the line in the past hour.

Stanley and Connie returned a half hour later and Ida told them that Uncle Andy had called. They looked very upset, and tried to send her to bed.

But her grandmother backed her up. "She's not mistaken, Stanley," she said. "I heard Andy too. I think you had better call him. He sounded as though he were ill."

Ida says she has never forgotten how shaken her father's voice sounded when he replied:

"Mom," he said, "Andy is dead. He hung himself three days ago."

Help from a Ghost

Donald Campbell was a famous Australian race driver. He was the son of another famed driver, Sir Malcolm Campbell.

After his father's death, Donald went on to establish his own fame. But for a long time, he missed the elder Campbell's advice and encouragement.

In 1964, he was driving a racing car on Lake Eyre, a dry salt lake in Australia. He was seeking a new world speed record. In one of the first of two mile runs, he had almost crashed. He still had the other run to go.

The salt track was breaking up, and he knew that the second run would be even more difficult and dangerous than the first. His crew was changing the car's tires. Sitting in his cockpit, Donald wondered if this would be a disastrous run, if he were experiencing the last few minutes of his life.

As the child of a world-famous race driver, Donald was very much aware of the extreme danger of the sport. Going through his mind at this time was an experience his father had had many years before while trying for a world speed record. A wheel had caught fire, and Sir Malcolm had narrowly escaped being killed. Donald had often wondered how his father had felt in the face of imminent death.

Now, waiting for his second and final run, this memory was uppermost in his mind.

One of the crew, Ken Norris, who was also one of the designers of the car, happened to look through the windshield and he noticed that Campbell was staring upwards intently. The driver's face had been filled with tension. Norris had a powerful sense of his driver's fear. But then Campbell's expression relaxed. He appeared now to be calm.

He then drove out and made a successful run.

Later, Campbell told his friend:

"It was the most incredible thing I've ever experienced. On the first run, I nearly killed myself. I knew the second run would be worse. I saw no hope at all.

"Suddenly I looked up and saw my father, just as clearly as I'm seeing you now. He was looking at me, smiling. Then he said, 'Well, boy, now you know how I felt that time in Utah when a wheel caught fire. But don't worry, it will be all right.'

"And he faded away. And indeed, it *was* all right."

The Ghost of a Deformed Monk

Maurice Maeterlinck was a famous playwright who won the Nobel Prize for literature in 1911. At the time, he was living in France, in a centuries-old building called St. Wandrille Abbey, once inhabited by priests and monks. It had been converted into a private dwelling. It was also reputed to be haunted. This did not bother Maeterlinck, for he was fascinated by ghosts, often referring to them in his works. However, he had never had a ghostly experience in the old abbey, until . . .

A number of guests were visiting, including the famous Russian actor/director Constantin Stanislavsky. An American woman was staying in another part of the house. In the middle of the night, the occupants were awakened by her screams. As the others gathered, she stammered that she had seen the apparition of a deformed monk.

Maeterlinck was not one to return to bed and let it go at that. Nor were his guests. They immediately made an attempt to communicate with the ghost through table tipping. And they were successful. The table rapped out a message from the spirit who claimed to be a monk named Bertrand.

"Oh save me, save me!" the table tapped out. There was a desperate tone to the message.

The listeners spread out through the building, looking for evidence. Stanislavsky found a plaque on which was inscribed in Latin:

"Bertrand: pax vobiscum: AD 1693."

Or, "Peace be with you."

Maeterlinck had heard there was a secret room in the abbey, and the company searched the place, looking for hiding places. Eventually, Maeterlinck found a hollow panel and pushed it open.

In a small compartment, they found the bones of a man who had been terribly deformed in life, and who had apparently died there, where he had been walled in.

A Terrifying Visitor

The two young military officers sat in a small apartment, completely unaware of the unusual visitor they were about to have.

They were drinking tea, relaxing from their duties. The apartment was part of a British Army barracks in Sydney, Nova Scotia. It was the afternoon of October 15, 1785. They were Lieutenant George Wynyard and Captain John Sherbrooke.

Suddenly Sherbrooke looked up and gasped. Wynyard followed his friend's gaze, and dropped the cup from which he had been sipping.

For the two officers saw a young man, about 20, standing at the door. The youth looked very ill. He was dressed in lightweight clothing, despite the cold Nova Scotia weather.

The young man entered the room and walked by the two seated men. Sherbrooke later described the figure as having "the appearance of a corpse." The young man glanced sadly at Wynyard and then, as the officers watched, spellbound, went through the doorway into Wynyard's bedroom.

Wynyard leaped to his feet. "Great heavens," he cried, "that's my brother!"

They rushed into the bedroom, but no one was there.

Communications were slow in those days. It was months later when Wynyard received a letter from India, where his favorite brother, John, had been serving in the British Army. The letter brought the news that John had died—the previous October.

Monkeys in the Closet

Beatrice Straight, a prize-winning stage and film actress, lived in New York City, but often spent weekends at a house that had belonged to her late parents, in Old Westbury, Long Island.

It was a spooky old place, with many Oriental ornaments that had been collected by her father, Willard Straight. He had been a U.S. consul in Manchuria, a region of China. He had also created a Chinese garden on the little estate.

Beatrice's thoughts were running to ghosts at this time, for she had recently appeared on Broadway in a scary play called *The Innocents*. It was based on "Turn of the Screw," a famous ghost story by the writer Henry

James. The story had been adapted for the stage by playwright William Archibald, who was also very interested in ghosts.

One weekend, Beatrice and her husband, Peter Cookson, brought a group of friends out from New York City, including William Archibald, to spend a country weekend. That evening, Archibald suggested that they do some table tipping. Beatrice recalls:

"Bill told us what to do, that the table would tip and tap out letters on the floor. For example, one tap equalled an A, five taps meant E, and so on through the alphabet. We went up to a bedroom my father had used and sat around a small table with our hands on top, and it suddenly started to go like mad, tipping and all.

"It said it was a spirit from the Gobi Desert. Sometimes the table would raise up above our heads, shaking, and then crash. We broke two tables that way. But before the second table broke, it spelled out:

MONKEYS IN THE CLOSET.

"I went to the closet in the room that I'd never looked in before. It was full of books that had been put there way back when. The table kept spelling out, MONKEYS IN THE CLOSET. I started pulling books out, and there at the back of the closet was an ivory statue with twelve monkeys on it. It was an ivory tree, and the monkeys were going up the tree."

By this time, everybody was getting pretty nervous. So when the table tapped out: BURY ME IN THE GARDEN, they thought that was a very good idea. They were eager to get the statue out of the house and out of sight. So the whole group took it out and buried it in the Chinese garden.

Half an hour later, Archibald went to his bedroom

and came out to say somebody must be kidding him. For on his pillow he had found one of the little ivory monkeys. But then everybody realized that the monkeys were not detachable. The statue was a solid block of ivory.

The next morning, they found another ivory monkey on the steps of the front door.

When *The Innocents* had first been produced, famous psychic Eileen Garrett had been engaged as a consultant. Beatrice now went to her and told her what had happened.

"She said to go back and dig up the statue," Beatrice relates. "She said don't do these things unless you're with somebody who really knows what it is all about, that there are spirits who are naughty and can cause trouble."

The next weekend, Beatrice and her husband went to the Chinese garden to dig up the statue. And there was no statue there!

5.
POLTERGEISTS? OR SOMETHING ELSE?

* Not all poltergeists come from another world . . .
* She thought the house was haunted by poltergeists—until the apparition appeared . . .
* Can a spirit leave the body—before the body dies?

When Is a Ghost Not a Ghost?

Hundreds of curious, fearful people surrounded the little house in Bridgeport, Connecticut. Some tried to burn it down, convinced it harbored a witch. Others threw garlic, an ancient protection against witches, onto the front steps. For very strange things were happening in this house.

It was occupied by Gerald Goodin; his wife, Laura; and their adopted daughter, Marcia, 11. They often heard tapping, banging sounds. Lights would go on and off. So did the TV. This was just a warm-up for terror.

Early one morning, Gerald Goodin noticed that a large refrigerator had turned from its usual position. The kitchen table began to flip up and down. Chairs fell over.

He heard a crash from his wife's bedroom. A religious picture had fallen off the wall. An even louder crash came from Marcia's room. Her bureau had fallen over. Wearing only nightclothes, the Goodins fled out into the street.

A policeman lived nearby, and he went into the house, but left when the refrigerator began teetering back and forth.

All sorts of explanations were offered—an earthquake, an underground stream, the house settling. Police came to the house to guard the Goodins. Experts on hauntings flooded in from all over the country.

Among them was a Connecticut man named Boyce Batey. He talked with many witnesses, and saw and heard many strange things himself. The turning point in his investigation came on New Year's Day, 1975, when he was sitting in the Goodins' kitchen.

A stereo set moved, and a table went up and down with a bang. Acting on a suspicion, he ran into Marcia's bedroom. The girl was lying on the bed, face down.

"That didn't seem right to me," Batey says. "When a loud sound is heard, the tendency is to go towards it."

A picture in the bedroom fell from the wall, scattering glass across the floor. Marcia still lay motionless.

Batey and other investigators began to develop a theory: the commotions were not being caused by a ghost or demon, they were being caused by Marcia.

It is becoming well known that some people can cause things to move without touching them. They can cause raps and bangs without hitting anything. This is called "parakinesis."

It happens particularly when people are emotionally disturbed. Often these people are teenagers or slightly younger, for this is often a difficult time of life. And Marcia had more than her share of problems. The Goodins had had a young son who had died. They had adopted Marcia, a Native American Iroquois from a reservation in Canada, in an effort to lessen their grief.

They were so protective of Marcia that she had almost no outside life. Batey says, "This girl was a very normal child. She was intelligent, artistic, gentle, sweet."

But she had almost no social contacts. Mrs. Goodin walked her to school and back. Some children taunted her about her Native American heritage. One kicked her in the back so severely that she was forced to stay home for weeks. It was when she was almost healed and was about to be sent back to her scary school life that the heavy poltergeist activity—things moving around—began.

Batey felt that initially it was Marcia's way of expressing anger at her parents and the world. Afterwards, she wanted to keep the excitement going and the company coming. The police in the house made a fuss over her. Her little game had brought social life into the house.

Batey recalls: "One time, Marcia and a policeman were playing a game of checkers, and he won. Within three minutes, a bedroom bureau fell over, and a TV set fell onto the floor. Marcia had been disappointed by her defeat, but was too gentle to express it in an ordinary way."

So it would seem that not all poltergeists come from another world. Some come from ordinarily harmless people who are very much part of this one.

A Fatal Apparition

When Arthur Koestler, a well-known writer, was a young man he was invited to a house in the Austrian Alps by a wealthy, very attractive woman named Maria Kloepfer, the widow of a German movie star. Soon after he arrived, she asked him if he believed in ghosts. He passed the question off with a joke. However, his hostess said casually that if he heard knocking on the walls at night to ignore it. She was plagued with poltergeists (noisy ghosts), she explained, but they were harmless.

He was soon subjected to more than mere noise. As they were sitting at lunch the next day, a large picture that hung on the wall behind Maria came crashing down. Koestler inspected the picture carefully and noted that the wire that held it up had not broken, and the two hooks to which the wire had been fastened remained solidly in the wall. He was mystified, but even more so by the fact that his hostess had not moved a muscle. This sort of thing was apparently nothing new to her.

When her aging maid came in and asked what had happened, Maria answered simply, "The haunting."

In a nearby village, Koestler heard vague murmurs about apparitions at his hostess's house, but he considered himself a rational person and paid no attention.

One afternoon, he and Maria went walking in the woods. Her small dog, Ricky, ran along ahead. Koestler described what happened:

"Suddenly Ricky stopped, rooted to the mossy ground, and gave out a growl which then changed into a plaintive, long-drawn howl. Maria also stopped and grabbed my arm. Her face had changed color, pale beneath her sunburnt skin. Her lips drew back and the braces on her teeth were visible. The wailing dog's hair was actually bristling. I felt suspended between horror and the giggles."

Maria turned and ran back towards the house, the dog by her side. "Now and then," Koestler wrote, "he licked her hand as if to comfort her."

Later she told Koestler, "Ricky saw my uncle approaching us. He sometimes sees him first and warns me."

She said it was the apparition of a dead uncle whom she had feared and hated, who had mistreated her as a small child. He had become insane, and had died when she was three.

Recently, she had begun seeing his ghost. She said that the apparition in the woods had appeared as a triple image—one coming towards her from the front and two simultaneously approaching from left and right.

Koestler left soon afterwards. A few weeks later, he heard that she had died in an institution. The elderly maid told Koestler that the apparition of the uncle had appeared on the veranda, and her mistress had had an epileptic seizure, from which she never recovered.

Pebbles from Heaven

Gilbert Smith and his wife and children lived in a small cottage in Western Australia, a dwelling that occupied the bewildered attention of millions of Australians for some weeks in 1955.

The mystery was pebbles. Pebbles raining from "nowhere."

This was farming country, and the Smiths, who were part Aboriginal, were engaged in growing flax. The land was owned by Bill Hack.

When pebbles began to fall on the Smith house, they thought it might be a joke. Mr. Smith went to his employer, Mr. Hack, to see if he might be able to deal with the situation. Hack did not take the matter seriously, but when he pulled up to the Smiths' house a pebble hit the roof of his car and bounced off, striking him on the shoulder. This, incidentally, was the only record of a person being struck by a pebble, though thousands of them fell.

During the time that Hack was in the house that day, many pebbles fell on the roof. Even more baffling, several landed on the living room floor, although there were no holes in the roof!

Word spread, and soon friends and neighbors gathered to surround the house with spotlights. They could see the pebbles falling on the roof and onto the surrounding ground, where they were standing. No member of search party was ever struck.

Some nights the groups brought shotguns and fired them into the air. They also brought dogs, who seemed as mystified as the people.

The newspapers sent reporters, who saw stones varying in size from a match-head to a hen's egg. They fell on the cars and on the floor and the furniture inside the Smith house. Some of the stones were warm or hot, others were not.

Bill Hack was concerned about the safety of the Smith family, so he drove 90 miles to the town of Mt. Barker and returned with a native witch doctor, Sammy Miller.

Miller suggested that the disturbance was being caused by the spirit of Mrs. Smith's father, who at the time was dangerously ill in a hospital. He had been taken ill while working near the Smiths' home. Mrs. Smith resisted this idea, but was startled when Miller went, without any direction from anyone, to a post hole not far away from where her father had been working when he had a heart attack. Miller said that at that moment the elderly man's spirit had left him.

The mystic said that when an Aborigine was close to death his spirit left him but it would linger about until the person died or recovered. He said there was no need for fear, that the spirit was a happy one and would not harm anyone.

Shortly afterwards, when Mrs. Smith's father died, the pebble showers ceased.

6. MALICIOUS GHOSTS

* A murderous ghost haunts a stairway . . .
* A doll takes on the anger of its owner . . .
* An angry husband gives his wife horrible haircuts—after he dies!
* George had always hated women—and after he died, he got worse . . .

A Dangerous Spirit

When Edd Schultz graduated from divinity school, he became a minister in an Episcopal church in Weymouth, a village near Boston. With his wife Caroline and baby Christopher he moved into an old house on the edge of town.

The house had two apartments on the second floor. There was a stairway between them that led down to the front door of the building. Although summer that year was extremely hot, the stairway was always very cold. It was something the Schultzes didn't think much about—at first.

But mysterious, frightening things soon began to happen. One day Caroline was standing at the top of the stairs, holding the baby. Suddenly she felt hands on the back of her shoulders, pushing her. With the baby, she fell 20 steps down the stairs. As she was falling, she could feel a cold chill around her, but she was aware of a warm glow from the baby in her arms. Neither she nor the baby were hurt.

A week later, during the middle of the night, the baby started screaming from his crib in a nearby room. Edd usually got up during the night to attend to the baby, but Caroline could not awaken him. So she got up and went to see what was wrong.

"As she was leaving our bedroom," Edd recalls, "I woke up. I had what I can only describe as a feeling of tremendous panic. I felt I was being held down by an evil presence. It was as though it was trying to possess me."

After a few moments, Edd managed to free himself and follow his wife down the corridor. She had been having her own experiences. She again felt icy hands on her shoulders. They closed around her neck as though trying to choke her. She broke loose and rushed to the baby's room. She picked him up and managed to calm him.

Edd recalls, "It was such a strong experience that to this day we prefer not to talk about it. It sends shivers up and down our spines."

Edd began to question the landlady about the history of the house. He discovered that the house had originally been a barn where a man had committed suicide by hanging himself from a rafter. His body had hung undiscovered for days, in the space that now was the staircase.

A Very Scary Doll

Can a doll haunt a house?

Take Robert, a large doll that for many years inhabited the Artist House in Key West, an island off the southern tip of Florida. The Artist House is a bed and breakfast establishment, a place to relax, but some patrons have had anything but relaxing times there.

The owner, Ed Cox, tells of a young German woman who stayed in the front bedroom, and who was terrified. "The more you go up that staircase, the worse the feeling is," she said.

The front bedroom was the place where the doll had been kept for many years.

A plumber working at the Artist House insisted that he heard the doll giggle, and that he found it sitting in different spots when no one was around to move it. Did it move itself?

Owner Cox tells of other disturbances in the house—of pictures that fly off the walls, for example. He once saw the door of a book cabinet spring open for no visible reason. Sometimes doors won't open. Sometimes they open when they shouldn't.

Who is Robert, and what could he be up to?

Robert was the doll of Robert Gene Otto, an artist who lived in the house all his life. When Gene, as he was called, was given the doll he was five years old. It was the custom around 1900 to give a child a doll that looked like him.

Robert the doll is the size of a child. He has human hair, and buttons for eyes. Gene used to dress the doll in his own clothes. He also gave it his first name.

Myrt Reuter, who owned the house after Gene died, cared for Robert as though he were a human being. "It has different kinds of clothes," she said. "It was in a pixie outfit when I got him. Now I have Gene's little sailor suit on him.

"I've been told," she said, "that when Gene did anything mean or hateful he always blamed it on the doll."

Myrt Reuter tells of renting the house to a law student one winter. She says, "He told this story that the doll was voodoo and it locked him up in the attic."

Was that true? Possibly. But it is a fact that many people have reported strange experiences in the house, whether or not Robert was causing them.

Enid Hoffman, who has written books about the Hawaiian mystical tradition, Huna, suspects that what is going on with Robert is what the Hawaiians call Mana.

"Mana," she says, "carries ideas. It can be stored in

certain things, wood and silk in particular. It flows in ways that are hard for us to understand. The doll has possibly infected the atmosphere of the house."

Psychic Carl Carpenter from New Hampshire tells how he once removed negative energy from a house. He had felt it was coming from a stone statue. He says, "I felt whoever made that statue pounded it out of rock, and got his anger out into that rock. You can put energy into an object, and that energy will affect people."

Gene had been a bad-tempered person all his life. The doll had been his "mirror image." A lot of his personality had gone into the doll—all the evil thoughts and actions. Possibly Gene's anger is living on after his death, through Robert.

The Demonic Hairdresser

It's distressing enough to get a bad haircut, but when it's a ghost who is giving it to you, it's an even grimmer experience!

That's what happened to a woman in North Carolina, whom we'll call Mary Johnson. Mary woke up one morning to find that her hair had been cut in a random, haphazard, disfiguring way. Parts of her head looked as though they had been shaved. Then it happened again—and again—sometimes even during the day. Mary would go into a sort of trance—she called it a spell—and when she came to, her hair would be cut.

Mary was about 60, and she lived in a small house with her daughter, Jennifer, who was 30. Jennifer began to wonder if she herself were being possessed by a spirit and were giving her mother these haircuts without knowing it. But sometimes Mary would go into her bedroom and lock the door, even nail it shut, and the haircuts would still occur.

The women began to wonder whether the haircuts were coming from Mary's dead husband, Roger, who was Jennifer's father.

Twenty years before, when the family had been living in Ohio, Roger had become involved in black magic. This terrified Mary, and she took the little girl and fled to North Carolina. Roger was bitterly offended. After a time, he followed and moved in with them. A few years later, he died of a heart attack.

Almost immediately after Roger's death, Mary and Jennifer became aware of strange sounds in the house. They heard knockings, footsteps, voices whispering. They saw vague, unrecognizable apparitions and soon the haircuts began.

Finally, in desperation, they called in a woman who was both a psychologist and a psychic. Dr. Jeannie Lagle is a well-trained psychotherapist whose work with clients often has an added dimension. She uses her natural psychic abilities to help her clients. She came to the house, talked with the women, and agreed that it was their husband and father who was causing the trouble.

"What we did was a sort of family therapy," Jeannie relates. "The unusual aspect of it was that one of the people—Roger—had been dead for some years."

The three women began meeting in séances, and, according to Jeannie, the spirit of Roger came and joined in. The séances were not an immediate success. Mary got at least one haircut at this time. But eventually the heart-to-heart talks seemed to calm down Roger's fearsome spirit. In the therapy sessions, Jeannie seemed to convince him that by remaining close to the physical plane and harassing his wife he was doing nobody any good, including himself. It seemed that he took Jeannie's advice and went elsewhere.

Whatever happened to Roger, the haircuts stopped!

The Ghost Who Hated Women

They say he was a terrible man when he was alive, full of anger and hate. He hasn't improved since he became a ghost.

They call him George, and he inhabits a bedroom on the third floor of the Old Stone House, a little museum in Georgetown, a section of Washington, D.C. The house is reputed to be the oldest building in Washington. It certainly seems to be one of the most haunted. The most violent ghost in the place is called George. He hates women.

The Old Stone House is a national museum, administered by the National Park Service. Rae Koch, the Park Ranger in charge, said that one time George tried to push her over a railing outside his third-floor bedroom. She managed to resist him, and lived to tell the tale.

Often, Rae says, when women try to go into George's room they can't get in. Something seems to be holding them out. Guess who.

George seemed to take a particular dislike to Evelyn, a teenage English girl who worked as a volunteer at the house. Rae says, "When Evelyn would go into that bedroom you could actually see her being pushed out."

There was something about Evelyn that seemed to set George off. And if you were with Evelyn, his anger might spill over on you. One time another member of the staff, Karen Cobb, went up to the third floor with Evelyn. Evelyn began to feel very uncomfortable, as well she might, and left the floor. Perhaps George was frustrated that Evelyn had gotten away.

"When Evelyn left," Karen said later, "the next thing I knew there were hands around my neck, strangling me. I managed to break loose and ran down the stairs. I ran outside. It was like it was pursuing me till I got out into the courtyard. I just collapsed on the bricks. My throat was badly bruised. I've gone up there since, but believe me, not with Evelyn."

Various visitors have seen George. One woman visitor asked, "Who is that man on the third floor with the suspenders?"

A staff volunteer, Peggy Beach, had ancestors who lived in the house before it became a museum. She thinks George is a great-great-grandfather of hers. He often wore suspenders.

"He was an awful man," she says.

7. GHOSTS WHO STAY BEHIND

* Colleen stepped into a time warp—of 50 years before . . .

* Place memories—the replaying of battles from long ago—are seen by thousands . . .

* She hitched a ride on his motorcycle, and then, after a few miles, she wasn't there . . .

* Do some ghosts haunt their old surroundings because they don't know they're dead?

* A gruesome, disembodied head discovered in the lap of an elegant theatre-goer . . .

The Lady and the Time Warp

It was nine o'clock in the morning on a day in 1963 in the White Building on the campus of Wesleyan University, in Lincoln, Nebraska. The corridors were filled with the clatter and chatter of students arriving for their first classes.

Colleen Buterbaugh, secretary to the university dean, had come over from the next building to deliver some papers to the office of a visiting professor from Scotland. She knew that the professor, James McNutt, wasn't in because she had phoned him, but thought she would put the papers on his desk.

When she opened the door to the small office, suddenly everything went quiet. She could no longer hear the noise of the students. In fact, the room itself looked different, somehow strange.

Glancing to the right, she saw a tall young woman with long hair. "It was puffed up," Colleen said, "like they used to wear before World War I. She was wearing a lacy blouse closed at the neck and long sleeves. A long black skirt hung to her ankles, and she was wearing old-time buckle shoes. She was going through a rack of music, apparently looking for something."

The room felt cold and clammy. Colleen looked out the window and felt she was in a different period of time. The tall trees were not tall. They were only a few yards high, as though they had been planted only a few years before. Across from the White Building stood the main library of the university, but it was not there now. There was no building there at all. Colleen felt she was seeing things as they must have looked on the campus 50 years before.

"The woman had her back to me," Colleen said. "She was reaching up into one of the shelves with her right hand and standing perfectly still. She wasn't at all aware of my presence. She never moved. She was not transparent, and yet I knew she wasn't real. While I was looking at her she just faded away—not parts of her body, one at a time, but her whole body at once."

Shaken to the core, Colleen staggered back to the building next door. As her coworkers gathered around to hear her story, an elderly professor said:

"Why, that's a dead ringer for Clara Mills as she looked when she started teaching here." He said that Clara, a professor of music, had begun teaching at the university in 1911, and had died suddenly in her office in 1940.

Colleen was shown old faculty photographs, and she recognized the mysterious, ghostly woman in one of them. It was Clara Mills.

After Colleen's experience, somebody asked James McNutt, the visiting professor from Edinburgh, if he now had any fears about going into his office.

"None at all," said Professor McNutt. "I don't see why Scotland should have a corner on all the ghosts."

When Battles Replay Themselves

Many a person has been frightened out of his or her wits while walking on a deserted moor in England and suddenly spotting a troop of Roman soldiers, in full gear, trudging along. The apparition usually fades quickly, but it's not something a witness is likely to forget.

Such sightings are a longtime tradition in England. After all, it was a couple of thousand years ago that the Romans were occupying the British Isles, and their apparitions seem to have been there ever since.

These spectres are sometimes called place memories. Somehow a scene has been impressed on the atmosphere and can be viewed at times. It is similar to a picture on a TV screen, for the ghosts never speak to, or even look at, the witnesses. They are not actually the spirits of these long-dead men, they are just images that can occasionally be seen by live people. They are not aware of any earthly surroundings.

One of the most famous of these place memories was observed by hundreds of people in 1642 in Warwickshire. It concerned the Battle of Edgehill, where 14,000 men fought in the English Civil War. Soon after the battle took place, on four weekend nights visitors to the battlefield saw the events "replay" themselves.

A pamphlet was published at the time, which described the scene as follows:

"A great wonder in heaven shewing the late apparitions and prodigious noyse of war and battels, seen on Edge-Hill, neere Keinton, in Northamptonshire 1642."

King Charles I sent representatives to witness these events, and they signed statements swearing that they had actually seen them.

A Hitchhiking Ghost

One day in 1978, a South African army corporal, Dawie Van Jaarsveld, was riding his motorcycle near the town of Uniondale. Suddenly he saw a young woman standing by the side of the road, waving for a ride. He stopped, gave her a spare crash helmet he was carrying, and, smiling, she climbed on the rear seat.

After a few miles, Dawie felt a bumping sensation. He looked back, and he no longer had a passenger. The spare helmet was strapped to the bike.

Dawie braked his motorcycle to a screeching halt. The area was treeless and there were no houses nearby. There was no cover for a person to hide. And he could see no one lying back on the road. The area was deserted.

Shaken, Dawie stopped at the first place he saw, a small restaurant. There were no customers, but an elderly man stood behind the counter. Dawie stammered out his story of the disappearing young woman.

The old man nodded. He reached behind the counter and pulled out a small photograph, which he held towards the young man. "Did she look like this?" he asked.

Dawie nodded his head. "Yes," he said, "that is her."

"That girl's name is Maria Charlotte Roux," the old man said. "A lot of people have seen her on the road, even given her rides in cars. She sits in the back seat, and then disappears.

"She used to live around here. She was killed in a car crash right down the road. That was ten years ago."

The Hotel Clerk Who Won't Quit

If you take a job at the Kennebunk Inn in Kennebunk, Maine, you've got to be ready to contend with a ghost. And it seems to be a ghost who doesn't know he's dead.

If you're a bartender, you've got to be ready to dodge mugs that fly off the shelves behind the bar. You've got to take it in stride if glasses shatter when nobody is near them.

If you're a waitress or waiter, you might have a full tray of dinners knocked out of your hand. Or you might set up a table and come back a moment later to find a mess—the tablecloth on the floor, silverware scattered, chairs knocked over. And nobody—nobody visible—would have been in the room but yourself.

The people at the Kennebunk Inn are used to this. "It's just Cyrus," they say, and they pick up the silverware or rub their heads where the flying beer mug hit them.

When Arthur and Angela LeBlanc bought the inn, they made a number of renovations. As we've seen before, this tends to stir up spirits, who don't like things to change.

One waitress, Pat Butler, happened to be psychic. "That's a ghost," said Pat, "and the name Cyrus keeps coming to me." So they called the ghost Cyrus.

One day a man came in for dinner. He said he had fond memories of the inn, because his uncle had been night clerk there for many years. What was his uncle's name, he was asked. "Cyrus Perkins," he replied.

Cyrus had lived in a room in the basement, so the inn was his home as well as his workplace. His spirit was very active in the cellar. John Bowker, a waiter, says, "You go down to the cellar, and he waits till you get your arms full and then he flicks out the lights."

Many employees of the inn refuse to go down to the cellar.

One summer, the LeBlancs' daughter, Elise, worked at the inn as a waitress. She became friends with two sisters who had come to the inn for a few days because they had heard of the ghost. They brought along a Ouija board, which is a device that supposedly spells out messages from spirits. But take warning, it can be dangerous to use. Sometimes it can bring in unpleasant spirits.

Elise says: "We took it down to the basement. The rule was no hands on the thing. We just held our hands over the board, about a half-inch above the planchette, which is the thing that moves around and spells out words. And it really moved! It was freaky! It scared me! I've never gone near a Ouija board except for that one time.

"We asked the ghost how old he was when he died. The planchette wouldn't move. I got an idea. I said, maybe he doesn't know he's dead. So we asked him if he was dead, and the planchette went to NO!"

A Sight Not on the Program

During the 1880s, a man and his wife were attending a performance at the Lyceum Theater, a well-known theater in London at the time. They were sitting in a box, which looked down at the seats on the floor. During the first intermission, the man happened to glance down, and he saw a ghastly sight.

A woman was sitting in a floor seat, wearing a flowing silk gown. The man looked again and then stared intently. For in her lap there appeared to be the disembodied head of a man! It seemed to belong to a person who might have lived a couple of centuries before. It had long hair, a moustache, and a pointed beard. The head looked deathly pale, as though it had just been chopped off!

The shaken witness pointed out the sight to his wife. Yes, she could see it too. The lights were just going down for the second act of the play. Even though the couple were fearful, they were even more curious. They left their box and went down to the floor to see if they could get closer to the woman. They were able to get close enough to see that the grisly object now seemed to be covered by a silk wrap in the woman's lap.

They went back to their box. At the end of the play they tried to speak to the woman, but they missed her in the exiting crowd. However, a sight such as this, especially the features of the head, remained fixed in their memories.

The man was a dealer in paintings. Some years later, he had occasion to travel to Yorkshire to evaluate some pictures. While in a stockroom, he unwrapped one particular painting, and gasped! For it was a portrait of the man whose head he had seen in the lady's lap all those years before.

Making inquiries, he found that the portrait was of a member of the family of the Earl of Essex. The Essex family had once owned the ground on which the Lyceum Theater had later been built. This particular man had been executed during the regime of Oliver Cromwell, a time when many aristocrats had met a similar fate. His head had been chopped off.

A part of the man—in both the physical and ghostly sense—had remained in this familiar site.

It is most doubtful that the woman in the theater had any awareness of the gruesome object she was holding in her lap!

8. BETRAYAL AND MURDER

* A ghost comes back for justice . . .
* A phantom follows her murderer . . .
* A ghastly deathbed scene replays itself, revealing a terrible truth . . .
* She said she'd never marry another man, and his ghost made sure of it!

The Ghost Who Came Back for Justice

Sometimes a ghost will stay in our physical world to see that justice is done, that its good name is cleared. Richard Tarwell was such a ghost.

Tarwell, a 14-year-old boy, worked in the kitchen of a large country house in England, in the year 1730. The owner, George Harris, also had a house in London. One day Harris received a message from Richard Morris, the butler of his country home. Morris said that the house had been broken into the night before and a large amount of valuable silverware had been stolen.

Harris returned, and got the whole story. Morris said he had been awakened in the night by a noise. He hurried to the butler's pantry, where the silverware was kept, and was confronted by two rough-looking thieves. With them, the butler said, was the young boy Tarwell, who it appeared had let them in.

Butler Morris said that the men had overpowered him and tied him up. Then they and the boy removed all the silver and left for parts unknown. Morris had been found by his fellow servants the next morning, none the worse for wear.

Some months later, George Harris awoke to see a young boy standing by his bed. He realized it was Tarwell. He presumed the boy had been hiding in the house since the robbery.

The boy said nothing, just beckoned. As the lad moved, making no sound at all, Harris realized he was seeing a ghost. He followed the boy out of the house to a large oak tree. The ghost pointed to the ground, and then disappeared.

The next morning, Harris had workmen dig where the ghost had pointed. They found the body of Richard Tarwell.

Police were called, and they interrogated the butler, who confessed. He was part of the robbery plot, having let the thieves in himself. While they were taking the silver, the boy Tarwell had heard a noise and investigated. One of the robbers struck the boy and killed him. To cover the crime, they buried Tarwell and tied up their accomplice, the butler, to hide his participation in the robbery.

Even though he was now a ghost, Tarwell was not going to let the butler get away with his death and the ruin of his reputation.

He was successful. The butler was hanged for the crime.

The Silent Witness

Many small children can see ghosts that the adults around them cannot see. Usually, they do not speak of these visions, for they have learned that grown-ups will rebuke them, will tell them they are making things up.

Irma was five years old in the summer of 1936. She and her family were staying at a resort hotel in the Canadian Rockies. One day two beautiful young people checked in. The man was tall and solidly built. The woman was short and slim. They seemed very much in love. The gossip went that they were on their honeymoon.

Irma was told they were champion swimmers, and had come here to put the final touches on their training for the Olympic games, which were to be held a few weeks later in Berlin. They would go off every day and swim in the surrounding lakes and rivers.

One morning at breakfast they mentioned that they were going to swim to a small island not far away. A waiter, who lived year-round in the area, overheard them and warned them to be careful. There was a very strong whirlpool near that island, with a powerful undertow. Over the years, several people had been drowned there, he said.

The young man merely smiled, and glanced about the table as if saying, "These local people always have their stories."

A few minutes later, they left the hotel in their swimsuits, laughing, as though they didn't have a care in the world.

An hour later, the man came stumbling back alone. He seemed exhausted, and in such a dire emotional state that he was weeping and throwing up. He gasped out a tale that his wife had been caught in the whirlpool and that he had been unable to find her.

The entire hotel was thrown into a frenzy of anguish. A search party was organized, but the young woman's body was never found.

Little Irma had a question all her own. For when the man returned, she could see his young wife standing behind him. She was wearing a wet bathing suit and was doubled over as if in pain. She was crying, "How could you? How could you?"

Irma tagged along with the search party, and all the time she could see the drowned woman behind her husband, tears running down her cheeks. Even when the group returned to the hotel, the little girl could see the young woman a few feet from her husband.

This continued all summer for Irma. She could stand on a high place near the hotel and look across the water at the island. She could see the young woman on its shore, bent over as though in pain, as though she had been hit in the stomach. And even at that distance, Irma could hear her cry:

"Why did he do it? I loved him!"

The Party Stopper

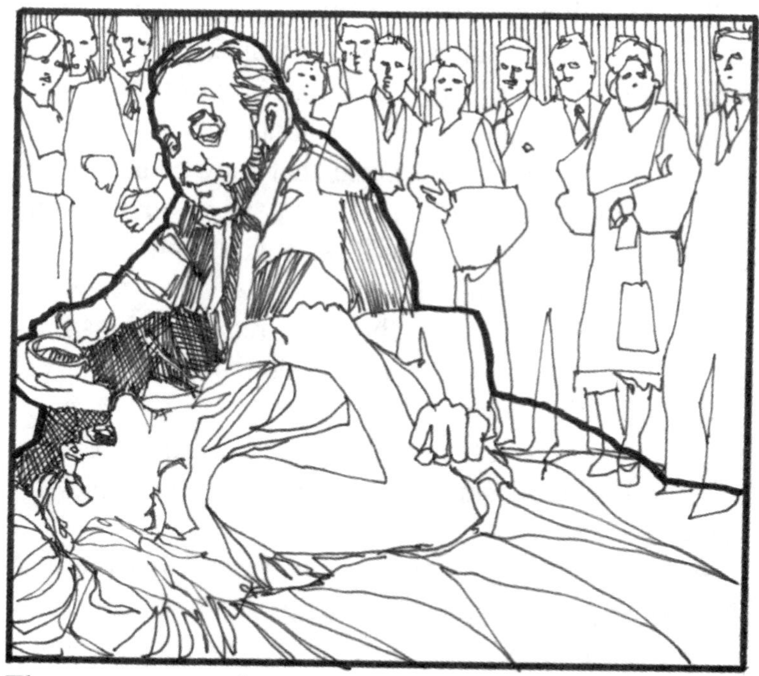

The young couple were throwing a house-warming party. They had bought the house, in Vancouver, Canada, only a few months before. The time was the 1930s.

They had bought the house from a middle-aged man who seemed in great haste to get away from the place. In any case, he was selling the house at a price well below its market value. The young couple were mystified as to why he would let this handsome house go at such a low price, but they congratulated themselves at their good fortune, and closed the deal.

As they made friends with the neighbors, they discovered that the man's wife had died in the house a short time before.

"Ah," said the young woman, "he probably was so

devastated by her death that he had to get away from these familiar surroundings, with all their memories."

The neighbor shook her head. "I would doubt that," she said. "Their marriage was collapsing. In fact, towards the end they seemed to hate each other."

The young couple moved in happily, but soon they felt an uneasiness in the place that they could not explain. They tried to ignore it, and went about doing renovations, tearing down walls, buying new furniture, putting their own stamp on the place. When they had completed their changes, they sent out invitations for a party, feeling that such an occasion would make the place more their own.

The party was fully under way, with laughter, banter, food and drink. A small band was tuning up to play for dancing.

All at once, an icy chill pervaded the living room. A frightened gasp went up from the group. A woman guest screamed, then another. For at one end of the room a ghastly scene had appeared. A silent scene, as though from a silent theatre.

On a massive bed lay a woman. She seemed struggling in the throes of death. Her eyes blazed with fear and anger. She appeared to be aghast, as though she had just discovered a terrible truth.

On a chair next to the bed sat a man. He was meeting the woman's glare with a small, tight smile, as though he were congratulating himself, and taunting her.

The young host and hostess gripped each other. For this spectre looked exactly like the man who had sold them the house. Many of the people at the party were neighbors, and they recognized the dying woman as the man's wife.

The vision was seen by the entire company for a brief—although seemingly endless—moment. Then it faded as silently as it had appeared.

The party ended instantly. The band was dismissed, the dancing cancelled. One of the neighbors, saying her goodbyes to the host and hostess, commented that this room had been the older couple's bedroom during the time they had lived in the house. The young couple nodded awkwardly.

Within a week, they had sold the house, including their new furniture, and had moved out.

The Waltz of Death

When the West was still wild, one of the few spots of civilization in New Mexico was Fort Union. This military post was manned by rugged soldiers and many young officers. They were very lonely, for there were few women in these parts.

One day a beautiful young woman, a niece of the commandant, came for an extended visit. Every man on the post fell in love with Miranda. This did not make her unhappy. There was little there to interest her except for men, and flirting was her favorite pastime.

One day a very young lieutenant, just out of West Point, was posted to the fort. He immediately fell madly in love with Miranda. For her, he was a new toy.

Fort Union was established to guard pioneers against the Apache Indians, who themselves were fighting to protect their homes and land. One day the young lieutenant was ordered to lead a small party against the Apaches. That night the young man pledged his undying love to Miranda. She answered in kind, hiding a yawn. As though playing a stage role, she murmured, "I will never marry another man."

"That is well," the young man said, "for whatever happens, I will come back and make my claim."

The scouting party was ambushed by the Apaches. Very few soldiers escaped back to the fort, and the lieutenant was not among them. Miranda showed little sign of sorrow. In fact, secretly she was relieved. Within weeks, she announced that she was leaving to marry a rich man back East.

The people of Fort Union held a going-away party. Everyone came in their best clothes. Miranda danced with one man after another.

Suddenly there was a bang! A door had flown open. A cold wind swept the room. A soldier's wife screamed and dropped to the floor in a faint. For a figure stood at the door. An unearthly cry came from its lips as it staggered forward into the light. It was the young lieutenant. His body was swollen, his uniform stained with blood. His scalp was gone. His eyes burned with a terrible light.

The figure lurched towards Miranda and took the terrified, rigid young woman in its arms. Faster and faster they danced! Miranda grew paler and paler. She slipped to the floor. The ghastly figure stood over her. The lights went out.

When the candles were lit again, the figure was gone. Miranda lay dead.

A few days later, a search party returned to the fort. They brought with them, over the back of a horse, the body of the young lieutenant.

INDEX

Aborigine belief, 60
Archibald, William, 51–52
Arkansas, University of, 23
Artist House, 64

Bari, Italy, 13
Batey, Boyce, 55–56
Beach, Peggy, 70
Bertrand, monk, 47
Betty, Aunt, 36
Bowker, John, 80
Bridgeport, Connecticut, 54
Building renovation, 32–34
Buterbaugh, Colleen, 72–74
Butler, Pat, 80

Campbell, Donald and Malcolm, 44–45
Canadian Rockies, 86
Carpenter, Carl, 66
Cave Research Foundation, 29
Cemeteries, 18
Charles I, King, 76
Chief, dog, 32–34
Cobb, Karen, 70
Cookson, Peter, 51
Cox, Ed, 64–65
Cromwell, Oliver, 80
Crystal Cave, 30

Dean, Lois, 15–18
Deauville house, 6–8
Decker, Lee and Pat, 9–11
Deike, Dr. George, 30
DeYorzo, Marina, 13–14
Dinwoodie, Wyoming, 27
Doll, Robert, 64–66
Dublin, Ireland, 35

Edgehill, Battle of, 76
Edmunds, woman ghost, 21
English Civil War, 76
Essex family, 82

Flyers, 37–39
Franklin, Fran, 23–25

Garrett, Eileen, 52
Gibbons, Harriet, 23–25
Glen Mills, Pennsylvania, 32
Good, Charles, 40
Goodin family, 54–55
Gulfport, Mississippi, 23

Hack, Bill, 59–60
Hairdresser, demon, 67–68
Halloween ghost tours, Toronto, 22
Harris, George, 84–85
Head, disembodied, 79–80
Hoffman, Enid, 65–66
Housecleaning, 6–8
Huna, Hawaiian mystical tradition, 65

Iannucci family, 33–34
Innocents, The, 50–51

Justice, ghost seeking, 84–85

Kennebunk, Maine, 79–80
Key West, Florida, 64
Kloepfer, Maria, 57–58
Koch, Rae, 69–70
Koestler, Arthur, 57–58

Lagle, Dr. Jeannie, 68
Lake Eyre, Australia, 44
Lamb, Reg, 38

LeBlanc family, 79–80
Lincoln, Nebraska, 72
Low Thunder, 27
Lupino family, 42–43
Lyceum Theatre, 81–82

MacDonald, Murdo, 22
MacGregor, Major, 35–36
Mackenzie House, 20–22; William, 20
Maeterlinck, Maurice, 46–47
Mammoth Cave National Park, Kentucky, 29–30
Mana, 65
McCleary, caretaker, 21
McNutt, Dr. James, 72–74
Mills, Clara, 73–74
Monkeys "in the closet," 51–52
Morris, Richard, 84–85
Museums, 20–22, 69–70

Nantucket Island, Massachusetts, 6–8
Nollamara, Australia, 9–11
Norris, Ken, 45
Old Stone House, Washington, D.C., 69
Otto, Robert Gene, 65–66
Ouija board, 80

Parakinesis, 55–56
Pebble showers, 59–60
Perkins, Cyrus, 79–80
Phone calls, 30, 42–43
Place memories, 75
Poltergeists, 53–60
Potter, George, 37–39

Race car driving, 44–45
RAF Shallufa, Egypt, 37
Reuter, Myrt, 65
Rommel, General Erwin, 38
Roux, Maria Charlotte, 78

Schultz family, 62–63
Sennett, Charlie, 26–28
Sherbrooke, Capt. John, 48–49
Smith, Margo, 6–8
Smith, Gilbert, 59–60
St. Wandrille Abbey, France, 45
Stanislavsky, Constantin, 46
Straight, Beatrice, 50–52
Strasberg, Susan, 12–14
Summer, Diantha and Mike, 15–17
Swimmers, champion, 86–88
Sydney, Nova Scotia, 48

Table tipping, 51
Tarwell, Richard, 84–85
Toronto, Canada, 20

Uniondale, South Africa, 77

Van Jaarsveld, Dawie, 77–78
Vancouver, Canada, 89
Victoria, Canada, 40

Warwickshire, England, 76
Wesleyan University, 72
Westbury, Long Island, 50
Weymouth, Massachusetts, 62
White, Dr. Will, 30
Women, ghost who hated, 69–70
Wynyard, Lieut. George and John, 48–49